EGMONT

We bring stories to life

This edition first published in 2010 by Dean,
an imprint of Egmont UK Limited,
239 Kensington High Street, London, W8 6SA

Postman Pat® © 2010 Woodland Animations Ltd,
a division of Classic Media UK Limited.
Licensed by Classic Media Distribution Limited.
Original writer John Cunliffe.
From the original television design by Ivor Wood.
Royal Mail and Post Office imagery is used by kind
permission of Royal Mail Group plc.

ISBN 978 0 6035 6519 9
3 5 7 9 10 8 6 4 2
Printed and bound in Italy

Postman Pat

Postman Pat and the Secret Superhero

EGMONT

"Da da DAA!" Charlie was zooming around the school playground in his red superhero cape.

"The superhero in my comic book can fly!" Charlie told Bill. "I wish I knew a real superhero."

"There's no such thing!" Bill chuckled.

"There might be!" said Charlie. "I bet there's one right here in Greendale — and I'm going to find him."

At the Post Office, Postman Pat and
Mrs Goggins were sorting the mail.
There was a big parcel for the Pottage
twins, and a special delivery for Charlie.

"Righto, Pat," said Mrs Goggins.
"I'm just popping out to see Dr Gilbertson."

Charlie and Bill were hiding in the bushes.
"Superheroes have to keep their special
powers secret," Charlie explained.
"We'll never find one if they think we're
looking for them."

"How can we tell if they're a superhero?"
asked Bill.

"Well, they will be very brave and strong,
and . . . WOW!" said Charlie. "Ajay is
pushing that train with just one hand!
He's so strong, he must be a superhero!"

But a few seconds later, Ted appeared from the other side of the engine shed. He was pulling the carriage with the Greendale Rocket!

"So Ajay's not a superhero after all," giggled Bill.

Charlie sighed. "Let's keep looking. There's got to be a superhero in Greendale somewhere!"

As Postman Pat set off on his rounds, disaster struck! He didn't notice that the back doors of the van had sprung open as he drove along the bumpy road . . .

. . . by the time Pat and Jess arrived at Thompson Ground, there wasn't a single bit of post left in the van.

"Oh no," cried Pat. "All the letters and parcels have fallen out. Jess, we'll have to go back and find them."

Meanwhile, peering through the surgery window, Charlie thought he had found his superhero!

First Dr Gilbertson disappeared behind a curtain, and Bonnie popped out, then Bonnie disappeared and Mrs Goggins popped out.

"Wow!" cried Charlie, "Dr Gilbertson just turned into Bonnie, and then Mrs Goggins!"

"Er, Charlie, I think all three of them were behind the curtain all along," explained Bill.

"Oh, well. I'm not giving up the search just yet!" said Charlie.

Postman Pat stopped at Greendale Farm to
check if Julia Pottage had seen any stray
letters or parcels.

"No, I haven't, Pat, sorry," Julia told him.

Nobody had noticed there was a parcel
stuck up on the roof!

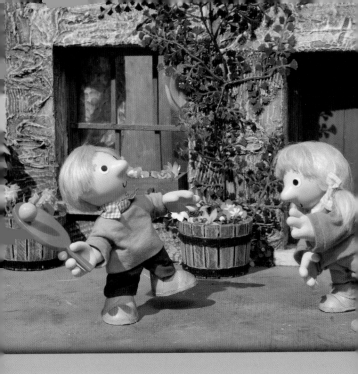

Meanwhile, Katy and Tom were playing a ball game.

"Let's see if you can hit this," said Katy, throwing the ball at Tom.

Tom hit the ball, it flew up into the air. The ball bounced on the roof, hitting a loose tile.

"Watch out!" called Pat. He caught the ball with one hand, and quick as a flash, moved Julia out of the way just as the tile came crashing down at their feet.

Suddenly, the parcel fell and Postman Pat leapt up to catch it!

The parcel was for Tom and Katy - it was a new kite!

"Pat!" exclaimed Julia, impressed. "That was really amazing!"

Charlie and Bill had found something
super too! As they walked past the
school, they saw Mr Pringle gliding
across the room.

"He's flying!" gasped Bill.

"My dad's a superhero,
and I never even knew!"
squeaked Charlie, rushing
towards the school.

Charlie and
Bill burst into
the classroom.

"Ah, hello boys,
you can give
me a hand putting
these pictures up!"
said Mr Pringle,
sliding across the floor on his ladder.

"Oh no, not again!" said Charlie,
disappointed. "Dad can't fly. He's just
got wheels on his ladder!"

Meanwhile, Pat was searching all over the village, looking for the lost post! He balanced on a bridge to pick up a bright yellow envelope, climbed up a lamp-post to fetch a parcel . . .

. . . and leapt over a garden fence to rescue some letters, just before Rosie the goat ate them for her tea!

Finally, there was just one more parcel
to find - Charlie's special delivery. It was
right at the top of the hill, hidden under
a hay bale. Pat gently took the
parcel, but when he
and Jess set off
downhill, the hay
bale started rolling
after them!

"Oh no! Run, Jess,
run!" Pat shouted.

Ted, Charlie and Bill watched in amazement as Pat and Jess raced down the hill towards the watermill, followed closely by a bale of hay!

"Look out, everyone," warned Pat. He tripped over a pile of rubbish in Ted's yard, and put his arm out to stop the hay bale - but Charlie's precious parcel shot out of his hand . . .

. . . and landed on the waterwheel.

Pat dashed inside the mill, ran up the steps, and leant out of the window. The parcel was just out of reach!

Pat jumped out of the window and onto the wheel. As he grabbed the parcel, the wheel began to move!

As the wheel turned, Pat ran faster and faster to keep up.

Then he somersaulted off the wheel, did a forward roll and landed on his feet.

"Wow!" exclaimed Charlie, wide-eyed.

"That was brilliant!" admired Bill.

"Thanks," said Pat modestly, dusting himself down. "This parcel is for you, Charlie! Special delivery!"

"It certainly is," joked Ted.

"Thanks, Pat,"
smiled Charlie.
"It's my new
superhero
comic book."

"I think you were right
all along, Charlie," said Bill.

"Yeah!" agreed Charlie. "There IS
a superhero in Greendale - SUPERPAT!"

Pat grinned. "Hee hee, I'm no superhero,
I'm just a plain old postman."

"Don't worry, Pat," whispered Bill.
"Your superhero secret is safe with us!"

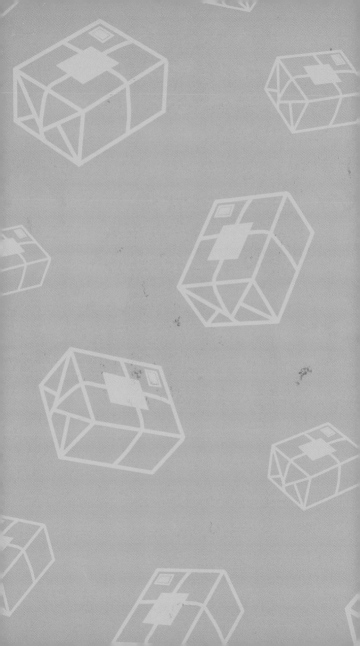